By Joan Walsh Anglund

TEDDY·BEAR·TALES

JOAN WALSH·ANGLUND

RANDOM HOUSE 🏠 NEW YORK

Library of Congress Cataloging in Publication Data:
Anglund, Joan Walsh. Teddy bear tales.
SUMMARY: Brief tales relate the adventures of teddy bears at play,
learning about colors, telling time, and traveling with Santa Claus on Christmas Eve.
1. Children's stories, American. [1. Teddy bears—Fiction.
2. Toys—Fiction. 3. Christmas—Fiction. 4. Short stories] I. Title.
PZ7.A586Te 1985 [E] 85-2238 ISBN: 0-394-87171-5 (trade); 0-394-97171-X (lib. bdg.)
Manufactured in the United States of America 1 2 3 4 5 6 7 8 9 0

A TABLE OF CONTENTS

For all the teddy bear lovers
including
Wally • Christine • Sarah
Ted • Lisa • Daniel
Teddy • Shirley • Justin • Julie
and
Teddy Maloney

and for all the dear and faithful
teddy bears
who have so staunchly
comforted and befriended
us all.

I never met a

TEDDY BEAR

I didn't like

A SURPRISE STORY

Teddy Bear
was going to have a birthday,
so his three best friends,
Peter Puppy,
Katy Kitten,
and Ruth Robin,
each decided to bring him a present.

They sat down
and thought and thought:
What would be the *nicest* thing each of them
could bring to Teddy?

One by one . . . they hurried away
to get their presents.

Peter Puppy wrapped his in red tissue and tied it with blue ribbon,
Katy Kitten used a calico-print wrap for hers,
and Ruth Robin put hers in a tiny bag
and tied it with pink yarn.

Then they all went off to Teddy's house
to give him their gifts.
Each of them thought privately,
"Oh, won't Teddy be surprised when
he opens *mine*!"

And Teddy *was* surprised!
For when he opened the packages
he found that
Peter Puppy had given him his favorite BONE!

And Katy Kitten had given Teddy her most
succulent FISH!

And Ruth Robin had brought him a
whole bagful of her
most delicious pink WORMS!

At first Teddy wasn't very pleased with his gifts,
but after a moment he realized that
each of his friends had given him
the very thing that they liked
the MOST!

So Teddy thanked them most kindly
and gave each of them a hug.
Teddy didn't want anything more for
his birthday.
He already had what he liked most—
three dear friends!

For Teddy Bear knew that friendship is the
best gift of all!

AROUND THE YEAR
WITH TEDDY BEARS

JANUARY

The new year begins

FEBRUARY

Valentine's Day

MARCH

St. Patrick's Day

APRIL

Easter

MAY

Arbor Day

JUNE

Wedding

JULY

Fourth of July

AUGUST

Vacation

SEPTEMBER

School begins

OCTOBER

Halloween

NOVEMBER

Thanksgiving

DECEMBER

Christmas

Little Bear
   has lost his ball . . .
      but who cares?

Little Bear has broken his chair . . .
   but who cares?

Little Bear
   is very hungry . . .
      but who cares?

Little Bear has hurt his toe . . .
   but who cares?

Little Bear
   has nothing to read . . .
      but who cares?

Little Bear has torn his trousers . . .
   but who cares?

Who cares?
    "WE DO!" shout his friends.
    "*We* care . . . and we'll *prove* it!"

So Betty Bunny helps
    Little Bear find his ball,

and Peter Puppy helps
    him mend his chair.

Katy Kitten
    bakes him a cake,

and Ruth Robin puts a
bandage on his toe.

Lisa Lamb writes him a story,

and Susie Squirrel
mends his
torn trousers.

And when they've finished each of their tasks,

they all have a party!
Because that's what friends are for . . .
to understand . . .

and help each other . . .
and, of course, to have fun just being
together!

TODDY BEAR AND I

Toddy Bear and I
    are the best of friends.
Toddy Bear and I
    do *everything* together.

Toddy Bear and I
wake up early.

Toddy Bear and I
brush our teeth.

Toddy Bear and I
eat our breakfast.

Toddy Bear and I
go out to play.

Toddy Bear and I ride our bikes.

Toddy Bear and I have a picnic.

Toddy Bear and I
take a nap.

Toddy Bear and I
go to the zoo.

ZOO

Toddy Bear and I
mail our letters.

Toddy Bear and I
do our shopping.

Toddy Bear and I
cook our dinner.
Toddy Bear and I
eat our dinner.

Toddy Bear and I
read a story.
Toddy Bear and I
say our prayers.

Toddy Bear and I go to bed.

A hug is the shortest distance
between two bears.

COLORS

Teddy Bear says:

"Red is an apple,
  yellow is a peach.

"Purple are the round grapes . . .
  high and out of reach.

"Blue is the tart plum,
  and an orange is juicy sweet.

"There, among the green leaves,
are rainbow treats to eat!"

THE CHRISTMAS BEAR

Little Bear had lived in the attic for so long, he couldn't remember anything but dust and darkness and the long years of quiet. But one day there were heavy footsteps on the stairs, and men carrying big boxes and talking and laughing. Then, suddenly, *everything* was being moved or packed away in boxes or swept out and thrown away.

It was moving day, and all was brightness and busyness in the attic! The Old House had been sold, and *everything* had to be disposed of before the new owners arrived.

At the final moment Little Bear was rudely lifted from the dark corner into which he had fallen so many years before. The last moving man to leave the attic picked up Little Bear by his leg and tossed him on top of a great pile of debris, and the moving truck departed down the long gravel-covered driveway.

Little Bear slowly blinked his eyes in the brightness . . . felt himself all over, to be sure that he was still in one piece . . . and,

with a quick jump, was able to hide in the bushes just before the garbage collector came to take away the last of the garbage from the Old House.

The first thing Little Bear noticed was how very cold it was out here in the outside world.

The next thing he noticed was how lonely he felt so far away from his familiar cozy attic. Then it began to snow . . . and snow . . . and snow! Soon it seemed the whole world had turned to a dazzling white . . . and Little Bear began to shiver!

Just then a great Snowbird flew by . . . and stopped to rest a moment on a pine branch above Little Bear's head. And when he heard Little Bear's story, the Snowbird asked Little Bear to come along with him. For, while all the other birds were flying south for the winter, Snowbird was flying north—as he *always* did, each year—to help Santa, in his workshop at the North Pole, get everything ready for Christmas!

Snowbird was Santa's messenger at the toy factory and speedily carried important instructions from place to place.

"Hop on my back," said Snowbird, and with a great flapping of his wings away they flew . . . up . . . up . . . through the dark, snowy night.

Oh, what a happy welcome they received many hours later when they arrived at the North Pole! All the elves came out to greet them, and Santa gave them each a warm hug. Mrs. Claus served them currant cakes and peppermint sticks and hot chocolate with whipped cream on top. But after a short rest it was time for work, because Christmas was very near and there was still so *much* to be done. The factory was busy night and day with elves and helpers hurrying to and fro. Bear helped by wrapping packages and painting toy soldiers and carving wooden whistles and even baking gingerbread cookies, while Snowbird flew back and forth overhead with urgent memos from Santa himself.

Everyone was busy at the toy factory. There wasn't a moment to waste. All the elves busily hammered and sawed, and stuffed and painted and polished, and tinseled and tied as they filled each order on every child's Christmas list . . . until at last the Big Night arrived! It was Christmas Eve.

The sleigh was packed and stood ready at the door. The reindeer were harnessed and eager to fly through the skies, but at the very last moment Santa's chief elf, William, could not go along to help Santa as he always did every year! William had the flu, and was so full of sniffles and coughs, Santa told him he must stay in bed! But oh dear! What was Santa to do? He had so many toys to deliver in just *one* night . . . Santa needed someone to help him on this very special night! Santa looked around at all the elves and helpers. They had all worked so hard, for so long, and they all looked so sleepy and tired! He couldn't ask them! There was only *one* pair of eyes that still looked bright and shiny and full of eagerness—Little Bear's. So Santa reached down and took Little Bear's paw and lifted him onto the great sleigh beside him. "I choose you, Little Bear, to be my chief helper this Christmas!

Hold on tightly.
Here we go . . . o . . . o . . . !"
shouted Santa. "Ho, ho, ho!
It's going to be a merry,
merry Christmas!" And
away they flew through the
velvety darkness, up high among
the stars.

All night long Bear and Santa filled the stockings of children all over the world, until at last, just before dawn, Santa's great bag of toys was *finally* empty! They had filled *every* order and checked off *every* child's name on Santa's long, long list!

But at that very moment Little Bear happened to look down . . . and there below, in a tiny tumbled-down hut that hardly had a roof, and no window or door to shut against the cold wind, slept a little golden-haired boy, in tattered clothes, huddled in the corner of a bleak and empty room.

There was no Christmas tree in *that* house! There was no stocking hung near that cold fireplace! There were no toys waiting for *that* little boy to find and enjoy when he woke on Christmas morning!

Little Bear knew how it felt to be alone in the world. He had been lonely and unhappy and without a home himself, and he certainly didn't want anyone else to feel that way . . . especially a little child! So Little Bear tugged on Santa's sleeve and said, "I want to stay *here*, Santa! I think this is where I belong."

Santa looked down and saw the little boy . . . and he understood. So he slowed the sleigh and hovered ever so lightly above the snow-covered shack as Little Bear jumped out.

Santa handed him the last of the candy canes, a slightly battered stocking full of tiny surprises, a bag of gingerbread cookies, and a tiny leftover pine tree with a bent star on top. Last of all, Santa took his own bright red woolly scarf and put it around Little Bear, and then he took off his great furry hat and put it on top of Bear's head.

"Thank you, Little Bear, for all your help," Santa said. Then he gently waved good-bye, calling back softly through the starry stillness, "Merry Christmas, Little Bear! I'm glad you found your home!"

Little Bear climbed down the chimney with his surprises. First he covered the sleepy boy warmly with Santa's great red scarf. Then he set up the tiny tree in the corner and straightened the star so it caught the last rays of the silver moon. Oh, how it sparkled in the moonlight! He found some bright holly berries on the bushes nearby and hung them as decorations on the branches.

How red and shiny they looked! The stocking full of surprises was hung by the fireplace and Bear started a cozy fire from twigs and branches he'd found. Finally Little Bear arranged the gingerbread cookies and the candy canes on the table, and then he lay down and snuggled next to the little boy for a few final pleasant winks of sleep. ZZZZzzz.

When the sun rose, the little boy stirred . . . and a smile came to his lips. He felt so warm, so cozy! "I must be dreaming," the little boy thought to himself, but it was such a lovely dream he didn't want it to end! So he kept his eyes closed and started to roll over, and then he felt something furry . . . and warm . . . and friendly! It was Little Bear!

"A teddy bear!" shouted the little boy, and he sat up and rubbed his eyes. Then he looked around at his little house.

"And a Christmas tree!" The little boy hopped out of bed and ran around the room looking at all the lovely surprises. The cozy scarf, the Christmas stocking, the cookies, the candy canes! But best of all . . . a teddy bear of his very own! Now he would never be alone again! He had a teddy bear . . . a Christmas teddy bear!

"Hurrah! It's Christmas!" he shouted happily. "It really is Christmas! And oh! what a lovely wonderful merry Christmas it is!" The little boy laughed as he and Teddy sat by the fire and hugged each other.

And it *was* the most wonderful, merriest Christmas *ever!* Because all you need is a little boy and a teddy bear to bring Christmas into *any* heart!